The Willing Walnut

This book is dedicated to Mother Nature.
May we always give Her the benefit of the doubt.

Leisel lived near a small forest in the hills of Northern Michigan. Wild animals, songbirds, and hardwoods embraced the forest as their own. Leisel often visited her favorite hide-away to share promises and dreams with her forest friends.

1

In winter and during the school months, the forest provided Leisel with warm shelter, always calming the

cold, strong winds

of winter with blockades of evergreens. Peacefulness engulfed the forest floor with a soft blanket of snow.

Leisel loved exploring the forest in winter, as each new day was another adventure. She valued the gifts of the cold season with animal tracks printed on the frozen tundra and thick icicles hanging from strewn branches.

5

Spring brought new life to the woods of winter and regenerated hope for Leisel's adventures. Leisel walked each path with the spring sunshine on her back. Birds, once again, returned to build homes for their young. Trees budded with leaves, giving life to their slumbering limbs.

For years, Leisel took in the sweet smells of spring. With the help of *warm sunny days* and chilly nights, rich sap began to flow freely from the trunks of the sugar maples. The mighty maples stood big enough for two, and sometimes three, spigots.

6

In summer, the walnut trees provided plenty of shade to all who wanted to picnic and escape the

HOT, BLISTERING SUN.

Leisel took naps under the hardy trees, their loyalty never ending, but forever changing with the seasons.

Leisel especially loved fall. The crisp air lit with a *rainbow* of color. A symphony of sounds filled the forest as squirrels prepared their nests and scuttled across the fallen leaves.

This was the time of year when Leisel gathered walnuts for her friends and family, just as her parents and grandparents had done for many years. She looked forward to Grandma's delicious walnut pies for the upcoming winter holidays.

Although filled with excitement for the coming walnut harvest, Leisel feared this year's gathering would be different. Sadly, the walnut trees, cherished for their rich lumber, had been hacked down all summer long.

During those summer months, Leisel saw the destruction of her special woods and sensed a disruption to her forest friends. Leisel's saddened spirit knew the best trees had been taken for lumber.

12

Nervously, Leisel set out for the annual harvest of walnuts. When she arrived at the battered slope, only one walnut tree survived the summer slaughter. The lone, thin tree had been overlooked by the lumbermen because of its crooked trunk and stubby tree limbs.

Devastated, she looked at the old tree closely and, to her amazement, she noticed the tree had an unusual abundance of fruit! The branches hung heavy, loaded to the point of breaking. Leisel envisioned the smiles around Grandma's table as the aroma of warm pies filled the house. Yet, as she looked closer, there was something strange about that OLD, CROOKED TREE.

13

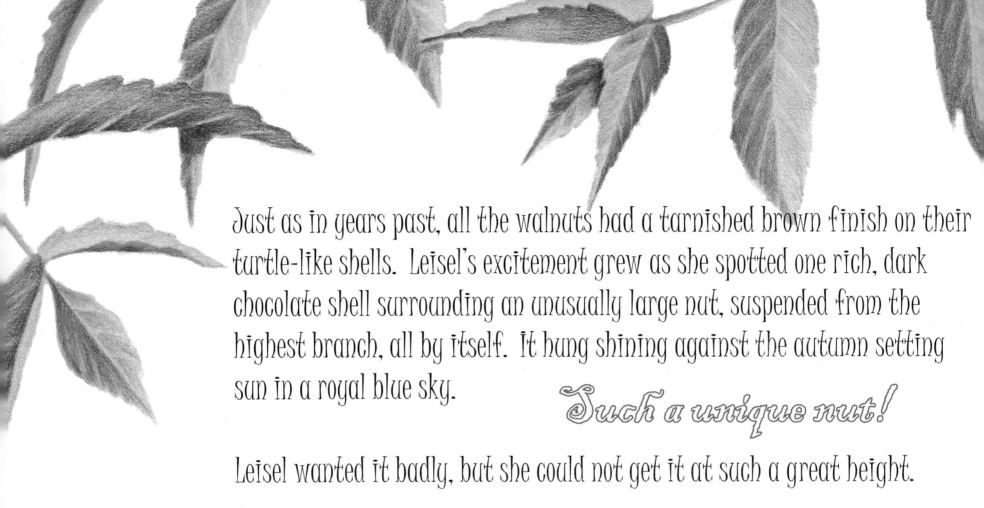

Just as in years past, all the walnuts had a tarnished brown finish on their turtle-like shells. Leisel's excitement grew as she spotted one rich, dark chocolate shell surrounding an unusually large nut, suspended from the highest branch, all by itself. It hung shining against the autumn setting sun in a royal blue sky. *Such a unique nut!*

Leisel wanted it badly, but she could not get it at such a great height.

Disappointed and unable to reach her prize, Leisel harvested what she could from around the lone walnut tree. Leisel wondered how one scraggly tree could produce so much fruit. Everyday, she joyfully gathered the walnuts that fell to the earth's floor and glued her eyes on the trophy that remained nestled on the top branch.

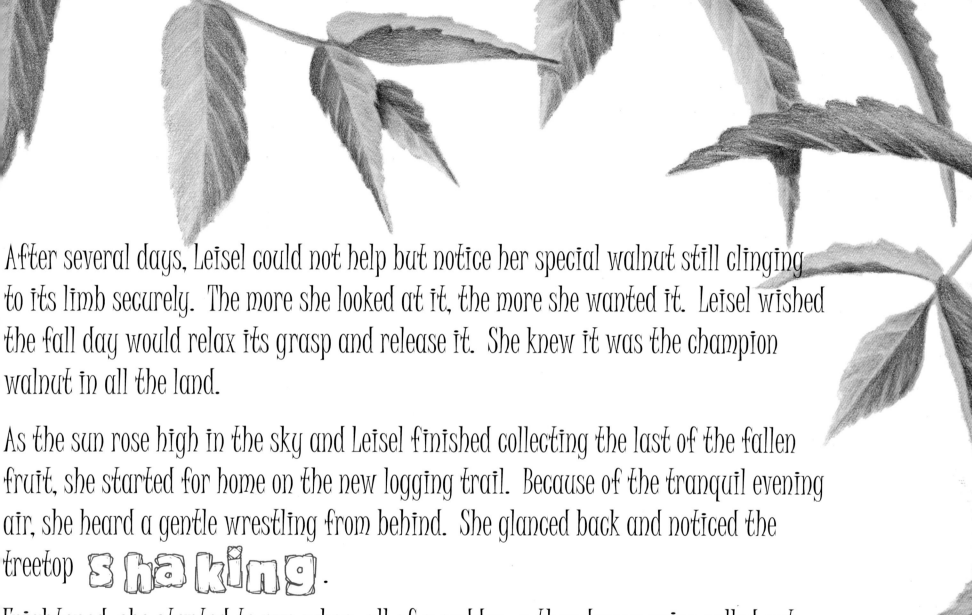

After several days, Leisel could not help but notice her special walnut still clinging to its limb securely. The more she looked at it, the more she wanted it. Leisel wished the fall day would relax its grasp and release it. She knew it was the champion walnut in all the land.

As the sun rose high in the sky and Leisel finished collecting the last of the fallen fruit, she started for home on the new logging trail. Because of the tranquil evening air, she heard a gentle wrestling from behind. She glanced back and noticed the treetop shaking.

Frightened, she started to run when, all of a sudden, a thunderous voice called out,

"Stop!"

The voice came from high above. The darkened walnut spoke.

18

Leisel froze in amazement. She put down her baskets and slowly moved toward the trembling tree. The talking walnut sobbed.

"What's wrong?" asked Leisel.

The walnut cried, "First, the lumbermen came. They savagely cut down all my ancestors. Look around, my brothers and sisters, mother and father, and all my relatives are gone! And now, you have come everyday to steal all my friends, hopes, and dreams. I am so sad and all alone."

"I know you want me too," said the walnut. "Come back tomorrow, and you can have me. But first you must promise me one thing."

"What is it you want from me?" asked Leisel.

"Before you go home, I want you to take the walnuts from your baskets, and bury one next to each tree stump. Return tomorrow, and I will be yours," vowed the walnut.

Trusting, Leisel carefully planted each walnut, hoping to bring back the lost joy of her new-found friend. With empty baskets in hand, she made it back to her home before dark. She told no one about the talking walnut, for she knew nobody would believe her.

22

Leisel woke the next morning eager and excited. After a quick breakfast, she hurried off in search of the talking walnut.

As Leisel approached the scarred slope, she heard the distant **growling** of a chain saw.

Nearing the crooked tree, her pace quickened with anticipation. All too soon, Leisel's joy turned to anguish. Much to her horror, she stood mortified as she watched a lumberjack cut down and haul out the last of the lone walnut tree.

Leisel walked over to the place where the tree had been severed. She sat down on the freshly cut stump. Fighting back tears, she noticed the dark chocolate walnut resting on a forgotten limb strewn on the ground.

25

It rested brilliantly in the autumn flowers. Now easily within reach, it was fulfilling its promise from yesterday.

26

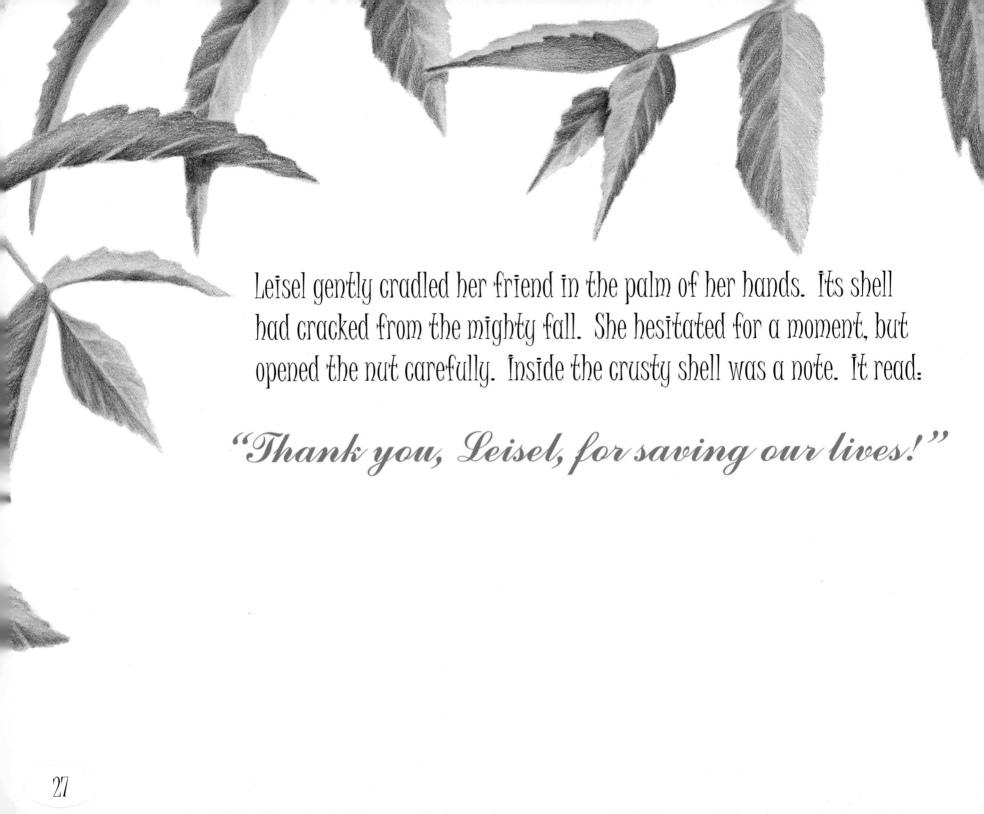

Leisel gently cradled her friend in the palm of her hands. Its shell had cracked from the mighty fall. She hesitated for a moment, but opened the nut carefully. Inside the crusty shell was a note. It read:

"Thank you, Leisel, for saving our lives!"

27

Today barren slopes seem lifeless, but tomorrow GREEN GROWTH WILL WIND ITS WAY UP through the forest floor. Because of Leisel, future children will have a place of peace and solitude in winter, new life in spring, summer shade, and Grandma's walnut pies.

First Edition

Library of Congress Control Number: 2008931513

Heintzkill, Tom and Elizabeth and Carlson, Jill Marie

The Willing Walnut

Summary: Leisel discovers the tension between nature and materialism while gaining a strong sensitivity toward the environment.

ISBN 978- 0- 615- 22267- 7

Fiction

10 9 8 7 6 5 4 3 2 1

Printed and bound in the United States by Color House Graphics, Inc. Grand Rapids, MI.

A Pakkers Publishing publication
Schoolcraft, Michigan

www.thewillingwalnut.com